HANS BRINKER

Library of Congress Cataloging in Publication Data

Betts, Louise.
    Hans Brinker.

    Summary: A Dutch boy and girl work toward two goals,
finding the doctor who can restore their father's
memory and winning the competition for the silver
skates.
    [1. Ice skating—Fiction.   2. Netherlands—Fiction]
I. Elwell, Peter, ill.   II. Dodge, Mary Mapes,
1830-1905.   Hans Brinker.   III. Title.
PZ7.E277Han   1988   [Fic]   87-15472
ISBN 0-8167-1205-0 (lib. bdg.)
ISBN 0-8167-1206-9 (pbk.)

HANS BRINKER

MARY MAPES DODGE

Retold by
Louise Betts

Illustrated by
Peter Elwell

Troll Associates

An early spring storm was brewing as Raff Brinker headed home. He had just spent a hard day repairing the dikes. These tall mounds of dirt kept the sea from flooding Holland. With its flat, low-lying land and many canals, Holland was in constant danger of being flooded. This was especially true during early spring when the snows melted and the rains came.

For most of the year, boats moved easily up and down the canals. But in winter, the surface of the canals usually froze over, and people would skate on the thick ice. They skated to work and to market, as well as just for fun. Children even skated to school!

Raff Brinker's mind, however, was not on the canals at the moment. It was on getting home before the storm broke. He was also eager to see his wife and their two children, young Hans and baby Gretel. Raff hurried along, and he was relieved to see the lights of his cottage.

"Papa!" cried little Hans when his father walked in the door. Hans immediately threw his small arms around his father's knees.

"I'm glad you're home," said Mrs. Brinker. "I was worried you'd get caught in the storm."

Mr. Brinker smiled and kissed his wife. The child in her arms gurgled happily. "Hello, little Gretel," he said to his daughter. Mr. Brinker took Gretel from his wife's arms and playfully tossed her into the air.

Mrs. Brinker knew her husband well and could see that he had something important on his mind. She had only to be patient, and he would soon tell her what it was. Outside, the rain started to fall.

As Mrs. Brinker prepared dinner, Mr. Brinker took something from his pocket. It was a silver watch.

"Take care of this until I ask you for it again," Mr. Brinker said, handing the watch to his wife.

Mrs. Brinker looked at the beautiful silver watch in her hand. She wondered how her husband had gotten it. Suddenly, Mrs. Brinker thought of the thousand dollars they had managed to save together. The money was meant for the children when they were fully grown. Mr. Brinker was keeping it for when that day would come. Mrs. Brinker felt uneasy.

"Dear," she said, "I hope you didn't buy this watch with any of the money we saved for the children."

Before Mr. Brinker could reply, there was a loud knock at the door. As Mrs. Brinker started to open it, the wind swung the door wide. The storm was raging outside. A neighbor stood at the door and called to Mr. Brinker, "The dike's about to spring a leak! Will you help us fix it?"

Mr. Brinker immediately put on his coat and headed out the door. It was the last time his wife and family saw him in his right mind. That night, he fell from the dike and hurt his head. The men working with him carried him home. When he awoke in his cottage, Mr. Brinker did not know where he was or who he was. He did not even recognize his wife and children.

en years passed. During that time, many doctors tried to cure Mr. Brinker. None succeeded. He merely lay in bed day after day, year after year.

By then, Hans had grown into a strong boy with bushy hair. He had honest eyes and a good soul. Gretel was graceful and kind, with sparkling blue eyes and rosy cheeks. Hans remembered his father as a great, brave man with a hearty, cheerful voice. But Gretel, who was very young at the time of the accident, knew her father only as the strange, silent man who lived with them.

Because Mr. Brinker could not work, the family became very poor. Mrs. Brinker earned a meager living by raising vegetables, spinning, and knitting. Hans and Gretel did whatever they could to help her. They worked outdoors and also cleaned the house. Hans earned money at odd jobs when he could find them, and Gretel sometimes tended geese for neighboring farmers.

Being poor, Hans and Gretel did not have the fine, warm clothes or the nice, shiny skates other people had. Instead, they dressed in layers of neatly patched clothes, and they skated on clumsy blocks of wood. These blocks were tied to their feet with thin straps of leather. Hans and Gretel never complained, and they managed to have as much fun skating as the other children in the village.

While Hans and Gretel were happily skating one December morning, a group of girls and boys came skimming along the ice on their way to school. Carl Schummel, a nasty boy, pointed to Hans and Gretel and said, "Look at the rag pickers coming down the ice! And look at their funny-looking skates!"

Hilda van Gleck, the mayor's daughter, replied gently, "They are patient children. It must have been hard for them to learn to skate on those strange things." Carl then felt a bit ashamed of himself, as Hilda left him and skated over to Gretel.

"What is your name?" Hilda asked.

"Gretel," she answered, "and this is my brother, Hans." Though they were nearly the same age, Gretel was startled at being spoken to by someone as pretty and wealthy as Hilda.

"Hans must have a stove inside him," said Hilda cheerfully, "but you should wear more clothing."

Gretel, who was wearing the warmest clothes she had, tried to laugh. But her lips trembled and her eyes filled with tears.

"My sister has not complained of the cold," Hans spoke up for Gretel, "but you are good to think of it."

"No, no," replied Hilda, quite angry at herself for hurting Gretel's feelings. "I didn't think. I wanted to ask if you were going to join the grand skating race in two weeks," she said. "You both skate well, and it costs nothing to enter."

Hilda went on to say that the prize would be a pair of silver skates. The girl's pair would have bells on them, and the boy's pair would have engraved arrows.

Hans and Gretel knew they could never win a race wearing their wooden blocks. Still, they thanked Hilda for asking and said they looked forward to watching the race. Hilda felt sorry for them. She reached into her pocket and held out eighty cents.

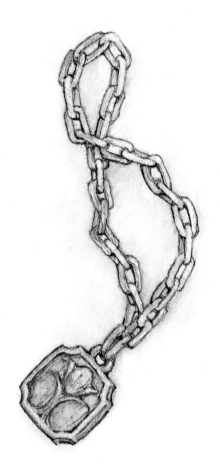

"This won't buy skates for the two of you, nor even one very good pair," Hilda said, looking at the coins. "But you can decide between yourselves who stands the best chance of winning and buy a new pair of skates with it."

Hans shook his head. "Thank you, but we cannot take your money," he said. "We haven't earned it."

Hilda thought quickly. She noticed a pretty, wooden chain around Gretel's neck. "Carve me a chain, Hans, like the one your sister is wearing, and consider this money as your payment in advance."

"I'll do my very best," said Hans.

Hans looked at the money in his hand, while Gretel jumped up and down. She was excited that her brother would have real skates. But Hans shook his head. "You must have a warm jacket first," he told her.

"Oh, please, Hans!" cried Gretel. "Buy the skates. I'll be so sad if you don't!"

Hans could not stand the sight of his sister's tears, so he gave in. "All right, Gretel," he said, "but *you* will have the skates!"

The next day, young Peter van Holp watched a young girl skating down the canal. She was wearing a red jacket and a patched petticoat.

"Look at her go!" Peter exclaimed to Carl Schummel. "She may well win the race!"

Carl sneered and said, "That little lady in rags is the special pet of Hilda van Gleck. Those shining skates are a gift, I believe."

Peter was happy to hear this, for Hilda was his best friend. Then he spotted Hilda on the ice and skated off to her. Hilda told Peter about how Hans had carved her a chain, so he could buy skates for his sister. Peter thought this was a wonderful idea and asked Hans to make him a chain too. Hans worked hard on the chain.

Two days later, he gave it to Peter, who gladly paid him for his work. That evening, Hans shook the hard-earned silver coins in his hand and prepared to go to the market to buy his new skates. Yet he did not seem excited.

"What's the matter, Hans?" asked Mrs. Brinker.

Hans kissed his mother, then cast a troubled glance at his father. "If only my money could bring a doctor from Amsterdam to see Father," he sighed.

"A doctor would not come for twice that money, Hans," said Mrs. Brinker. "Besides, it would do no good if he did." She had spent much money on doctors before, but nothing had helped. "It seems your father's illness is permanent," she said. "Go and buy the skates, Hans."

Hans felt sad as he started to skate toward the town of Amsterdam. But skating always lifted his spirits, and soon he was whistling down the canal on his wooden blocks. Suddenly, he saw a familiar face skating toward him. Why, it was the great Dr. Boekman, the most famous physician and surgeon in all of Holland! Hans had never met this man, but he had seen his picture in many store windows.

The doctor was tall and thin, and had a stern look. Ordinarily, Hans would have felt too shy to approach him. But this was one of the greatest doctors in the world, and perhaps this man could help Hans's father.

"Dr. Boekman, sir!" Hans called out.

The great man stopped and turned around. Thinking Hans was a poor beggar, the doctor scowled. "What do you want?" he asked.

"It's my father—can you help him?" asked Hans, show-ing the silver coins in his hand. He then explained his father's condition as best he could, occasionally wiping away a tear. Oddly enough, the doctor's expression changed. His face softened and his eyes looked kind. He placed a gentle hand on Hans's shoulder and asked him to put away his money.

"Your father fell ten years ago? Hmmm," the doctor said, deep in thought. "It sounds like a bad case, but I will see him. I'll come by in a week, when I return from the city of Leyden."

"Oh, thank you, sir!" said Hans.

The two said good-bye. Dr. Boekman was still think-ing as he skated away. The case is probably hopeless, he thought to himself, but I like the boy. He reminds me of my long-lost son, Laurens!

Hans, filled with relief and hope, whistled all the way to Amsterdam, where he purchased a fine new pair of skates.

After returning home, Hans tried out his new skates near the cottage. Gretel soon joined him on her skates. The two of them marveled at being able to glide, jump, and swirl on the shiny metal blades. Suddenly, they heard a scream coming from the cottage. Though the scream was not loud, Hans and Gretel knew its meaning all too well.

"Come on, Gretel!" cried Hans. "Father's frightening Mother!"

Hans and Gretel tore off their skates, slipped into their shoes, and ran toward the house.

No one else on the canal that evening knew about the troubles at the Brinker cottage. In fact, the canal was especially lively with the merry shouts of children, for the Christmas holiday had just begun.

Among the frolicking skaters was a group of six teenage boys talking excitedly among themselves. They were planning a skating journey to The Hague, a beautiful Dutch city fifty miles away near the North Sea.

"We'll leave as soon as the sun comes up tomorrow," said Peter van Holp, the leader for the trip. Peter's younger brother, Ludwig, was also part of the group.

Carl Schummel, despite his bad temper, was included as well. This made him feel overly proud, and he looked at plump Jacob Poot and frowned. "I don't think you'll be able to keep up with us, Jacob," Carl said.

"Of course I will!" exclaimed Jacob. His face was red from the cold, but it was redder still from embarrassment.

"Besides, I've promised Ben. What better way to show our country to an Englishman?"

The boys looked over at Jacob's English cousin, Ben Dobbs, who turned to Lambert van Mounen for a translation. Lambert was smart, a good skater, and the only one of them who could speak English.

Lambert translated for Ben, while Peter said, "We make a fine team! We'll all go to The Hague!"

"Hurray! To The Hague!" the boys cheered.

It was barely light when the boys set off the following morning. Peter stumbled over a log on the side of the canal, but otherwise the skaters started off well. After skating hard for several hours, they stopped for a bite to eat. It was then that Peter discovered he had lost the leather pouch containing all of the group's money. Without money they had no choice but to turn back.

When the boys arrived back home, Carl was in a bad mood. Spotting Hans on the ice, he said snidely, "Well, well, well. If it isn't that Hans Brinker in the patched leather breeches."

Peter looked for Hans among the skaters. "Ah, there he is! Hmmm, I wonder what's the matter with him." Peter skated over to him quickly. Hans looked pale and worried.

"Hello, Hans Brinker!" Peter called out.

Hans smiled. "Hello! It's a good thing you stopped me. Is this yours?" Hans asked, showing Peter the missing pouch.

"Hurray!" shouted all the boys except Carl, who scowled.

Peter thanked Hans. He then drew him away from the others and asked, "How did you know it was mine?"

"I saw your pouch when you paid me for making the chain," Hans replied. "I was skating this morning and tripped over some pieces of wood. That's when I saw your pouch hidden under a log."

"I must have dropped it when I stumbled there this morning," said Peter.

Hans would not take any reward for finding the money, but he did tell Peter why he was worried. "It's my father. He lost his mind many years ago. Last night, he pushed Mother as she kneeled to keep the fire going. My sister, Gretel, and I were skating when we heard Mother scream. We ran in and saw Mother's dress on fire.

"I tried to put out the fire," Hans continued, "but Father kept pushing me away. All that time he laughed. It was a terrible laugh. To calm him down, Gretel put out a bowl of food for him. That's when he left Mother and went to the food. Luckily, Mother wasn't burned. But she thinks Father's illness is getting much worse. That's why I'm going to Leyden to find Dr. Boekman."

"Dr. Boekman!" exclaimed Peter. "Why, he's the meanest man in Holland!"

"He looks mean, but his heart is kind," said Hans. "He promised to come in a week. But if he knew my father may be dying, he might come sooner."

This gave Peter an idea. "I'm going to Leyden myself and could deliver the message for you," he said.

Hans was grateful for this, because he did not like leaving his mother and sister alone. He thanked Peter, who once more offered him some money for finding the pouch. Hans shook his head and said he would rather find work somewhere in town.

"Now that you mention it," said Peter, "my father is looking for someone to carve a door for our new summer house. Just tell my father you are the Hans Brinker I told him about," said Peter. "He liked the chain you carved for my sister. I'm sure he will be glad to see you and give you work."

Hans was surprised and grateful. "Thank you!" he said.

Peter's group wanted to go eat, and Hans was eager to get back home. So the two boys said good-bye and departed.

After lunch, the group of six boys began their skating trip again. By now, the canal was crowded with skaters. There were fashionable ladies from Leyden, fish-wives from nearby villages, young women who carried babies in bright shawls on their backs, and old women with baskets on their heads. Boys and girls chased each other, hiding behind one-horse sleds loaded with timber and peat. Older men skated while smoking their pipes.

After several miles, the canal fed into a frozen lake. There iceboats of all shapes and sizes glided swiftly about. Ben, who had never seen iceboats, skated closer for a better look. The boats had sails that were much larger than those on ordinary boats. The iceboats had rudders for guiding and brakes for stopping.

Ben was delighted at the sight—until a huge iceboat under full sail came tearing down the canal right toward him! The boat's prow rapidly drew closer, while the skipper shouted from the deck. Frozen with fear, Ben could neither move nor shut out the ringing in his ears. Suddenly, he found himself spinning some distance behind the boat. It had passed within an inch of his shoulder, but he was safe!

The boys were quite shaken by Ben's near-accident and stopped to rest a few minutes. After a while, they were skating up the canal with renewed energy. Jacob, however, was beginning to lag behind. He tried his best not to seem tired. But before long, his stout body grew heavier and heavier, his tottering legs weaker and weaker, until he could go no farther.

"That's all right," said Peter when Jacob admitted his

fatigue. "We can take an iceboat the rest of the way to Leyden." The other boys cheerfully agreed, each secretly glad to stop skating too.

When they arrived at Leyden, the boys' stomachs were howling with hunger. Quickly they found an inn called the Red Lion where they could eat. There they had their fill of rye bread, sauerkraut, potato salad, and herring. Afterward, they accepted the owner's suggestion to spend the night at the Red Lion.

Right after dinner, while most of the group walked around the city, Peter and Jacob went to find Dr. Boekman to deliver Hans's message. They checked several inns, but the best they could do was to leave a note for the doctor at the inn where he usually stayed.

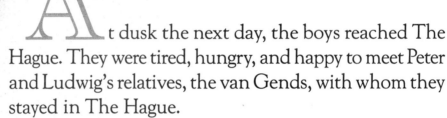

At dusk the next day, the boys reached The Hague. They were tired, hungry, and happy to meet Peter and Ludwig's relatives, the van Gends, with whom they stayed in The Hague.

The next three days were filled with surprises and wonder, as the boys explored The Hague. They went to an art gallery and The Hague's fine museum. The boys went horseback riding with Mr. van Gend and tramped about the city on foot. They saw the zoo and the park. They watched the workers on the docks loading cheese and herring from canal boats and into warehouses. By the end of their stay, there was hardly a store, museum, or historic building the boys hadn't seen, and hardly a cobblestone they had not walked upon.

On their fourth morning at the van Gends', the boys thanked their hosts and said good-bye.

As they turned homeward, the boys' thoughts turned to the upcoming grand skating race. Suddenly, they imagined they were in the race just then. No one said anything as they all sped forward. The only sound was that of blades scraping against the ice. With body bent low and eager eyes, each boy did his best, whizzing by the gentle skaters on the canal.

Gradually, the boys slowed down except for Peter and Ben. They were the only two left, racing neck and neck. The rest of the boys started shouting excitedly: "Peter's ahead!" "No, Ben is!" "Look at them go!" "Now they're at the turn." "Peter's ahead—it looks like he won." "Hurray! Good for Peter!"

The turn in the canal was evidently Peter and Ben's goal, for the two racers came to a sudden halt after passing it. The other boys skated up to them and congratulated both for an exciting race.

Going home, the boys passed through Leyden again. Peter looked for Dr. Boekman and learned that he had left for the Brinkers' house already. After that, it seemed the boys were back home in no time, safe and sound.

The next day, Dr. Boekman and his assistant arrived at the Brinker cottage. They examined Hans's father and discussed what should be done. "We could operate today," said Dr. Boekman to Hans. "But I must warn you that the operation is risky. It could just as easily kill him as cure him." Seeing the fear in Hans's eyes, he quickly added, "I believe, though, that the operation will cure him. I'll wait while you talk it over with your mother."

Trembling, Hans told his mother and sister what the doctor had said. Mrs. Brinker listened carefully, but Gretel was too frightened to understand.

Mrs. Brinker looked over at her husband, lying in pain. She loved him so much and wanted him to be cured! Not knowing what to do, she searched her heart for an answer. A moment later, she said calmly, "It is right, Doctor. You have my consent for the operation."

Immediately, the doctor opened up his leather case and drew out one sharp instrument after another. Gretel shrieked at the sight and ran out of the cottage. She threw herself on the cold, snowy ground and cried as if her heart would break. Gretel lay there for some time, shivering in the snow and gradually growing sleepy. She knew she should get up if she didn't want to freeze. But Gretel was too tired to move.

Suddenly, a firm hand was shaking her awake. Gretel opened her eyes and thought she must be dreaming. There was Hilda van Gleck, shaking her and begging her to get up. Hilda then helped Gretel to her feet.

"Here," Hilda said, "lean against me. Keep moving and you'll get warm. Let me take you back to your cottage."

Gretel exclaimed that she could not go back to the

cottage—not while the doctor was there, not when her father could be dying.

Tears of sympathy glistened in Hilda's eyes.

"Why, Hilda, are you crying for us?" Gretel asked. It made her feel better to see how much Hilda cared. Gretel now tried to cheer Hilda. "Oh, I know Father will be cured now!" said Gretel, peering through the window. "He's lying very still with a bandage on his head. Everyone is looking at him. Oh, I must go to my mother!" Gretel hugged Hilda, thanked her, and dashed away.

Hilda stayed outside the Brinker cottage for some time, even though she knew she would be late for school. What was happening inside was a miracle! Mr. Brinker had awakened at last! She heard Mrs. Brinker laugh, and Hans and Gretel cry out, "Here we are, Father!" Tears of happiness trickled down Hilda's cheeks.

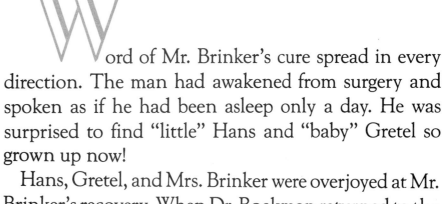

Word of Mr. Brinker's cure spread in every direction. The man had awakened from surgery and spoken as if he had been asleep only a day. He was surprised to find "little" Hans and "baby" Gretel so grown up now!

Hans, Gretel, and Mrs. Brinker were overjoyed at Mr. Brinker's recovery. When Dr. Boekman returned to the Brinker cottage the next day, he noticed how cozy and comfortable the little house felt.

The doctor asked a few questions and felt his patient's pulse. "He is still very weak and must have more food. What he needs is fresh meat, bread, and more blankets. He looks cold."

Hearing this, Mrs. Brinker was troubled. She could barely afford black bread and porridge, let alone more blankets. "If only we knew where the lost money was!" sighed Mrs. Brinker after the doctor had left. "How could our one thousand dollars have disappeared?"

"Maybe it's finally time to sell the silver watch," said Hans, reminding her of the watch her husband had given her so long ago for safekeeping. Suddenly, Hans had an idea. "Now that Father is well," he said, "why not ask him where the watch came from?"

Mrs. Brinker agreed. But just then Hilda van Gleck and a maid knocked on the door. They had brought meat, jelly, and a whole basket full of bread! Then the doctor sent a man with a wagon from town who brought more of all that, plus a fine bed and blankets.

"He will get well now, thanks to them!" cried Mrs. Brinker.

That evening, Hans quietly asked if his father had spoken of the missing money. Mrs. Brinker shook her head and replied, "He hasn't said a word about it. I don't think he remembers anything about the thousand dollars."

"Thousand dollars?" echoed a faint voice from the bed.

Hans and Mrs. Brinker were startled. Mrs. Brinker got up from her seat, ready to ask her husband where he had put the money. Hans stopped her. "Remember," he said, "the doctor told us not to upset Father." Hans went over to his father's bedside.

"It's lucky I told you where I buried the money," Mr. Brinker said. "I'd feel terrible if I'd left you here without it for all those years."

Mrs. Brinker choked back her sobs, while Hans said gently, "I was so young when you fell, Father. I never knew the story of the buried money."

"Then I'll tell you, my boy," said Mr. Brinker. "It was just before dawn on the same day I was hurt. The evening before, my partner had said something that made me distrust him. He was the only one besides your mother who knew we had saved a thousand dollars. So I rose very early in the morning and buried the money!"

"Well, how about that!" said Hans, motioning Gretel and Mrs. Brinker to stay quiet. "But I bet you've forgotten where you buried it!"

"No, I remember well. It was close by the willow sapling behind the cottage," Mr. Brinker said sleepily. "On the south side."

Later that night, Hans and his mother dug in all directions around the tree, but the money was not there.

Hans spent all the next day in Amsterdam looking for work. It seemed none was to be found anywhere. Then Hans remembered Peter van Holp's suggestion that Hans ask Peter's father about carving the van Holp's summer house doors. Hans called at the van Holp's house, where the family received him warmly. As luck would have it, Mr. van Holp wanted Hans to start working immediately!

That evening, Hans returned home lighthearted. From outside the cottage, he could see Gretel inside with their friend, Annie, who lived nearby. "Hurray!" he shouted. "I found work!" The girls ran out to greet him.

Hans told them about his new job and the three chatted excitedly. Annie was seated on a tree stump, while the other two stood before her. This arrangement gave Annie an idea. "Let's play a game," she said. She leaned down and picked up a stick. "This is my magic wand," Annie said, "and I'm your fairy godmother. Now each of you gets one wish. What is yours, Hans?"

A serious look swept over Annie's face as she looked up at him. Annie truly wished she could have a fairy's power. For a moment, even Hans felt that Annie really could bring about magic.

"I wish," said Hans solemnly, "that I could find what Mother and I were looking for last night."

Gretel laughed merrily as the fairy godmother sprang up, stamped her foot three times, and said, "Your wish is granted!" Hans desperately wanted to believe it would come true. Before she could grant Gretel's wish, though, Annie was called home.

"Goodnight, mortals!" she said.

"Goodnight, fairy godmother!" Hans and Gretel said again and again.

Hans and Gretel were laughing as they went inside. But just as Hans stepped into the cottage, he stopped. "I've got it!" he cried. Quickly grabbing a spade, Hans plunged back outside and began to dig. "Mother! Gretel! Come here!" he started shouting. But Hans's shouts were unnecessary, for his sister and mother were at his side in a second.

"I see now! We dug at the wrong tree last night!" he said, digging furiously. "We cut down the willow tree last spring. The money should be by this stump!"

Sure enough, Hans dug up from the ground an old stone pot. In it was a stocking and pouch filled with the long-lost money!

With the lost money now recovered, only the mystery of the silver watch remained. One afternoon, Mrs. Brinker handed the watch to her husband and urged him to explain how he had acquired it. Mr. Brinker turned the watch over and over in his hand. "I hesitate to say," said Mr. Brinker sadly. "Seems like I'd be telling the secrets of the dead. The lad who gave me the watch was very troubled at the time. He said he had killed someone, but I couldn't believe it. He was as fresh and honest-looking as our Hans. He came up to me suddenly and said, 'I've done something terrible. I never meant to, but the man is dead. I must flee Holland!'

"The lad then took hold of my arm and gave me his watch," Mr. Brinker continued. "He asked me to give the watch to his father in a week and to tell him his son had sent it. If the father wanted the son back, he was to write a letter to a boy in some faraway town. But I can't remember what boy or the name of the town!"

"Do you remember the father's name?" Mrs. Brinker asked.

Mr. Brinker thought hard, but no name came to mind. The only clue they had was the initials on the back of the watch: "L.J.B." The Brinkers, however, could not think of anyone whose name fit those initials.

"Maybe Dr. Boekman will know," suggested Mrs. Brinker. "He sees so many people."

On Dr. Boekman's next visit, Mrs. Brinker showed the watch to him. "Where did you get this?" he exclaimed. As Mrs. Brinker told him the story, tears rolled down the doctor's face. "Laurens! My Laurens! This is my son's watch!"

Trembling with joy, the doctor sat down and explained what had happened. "Laurens was my assistant," Dr. Boekman began, "and by mistake one day he poured poison instead of medicine for one of my patients. Luckily, I discovered the error before the man drank it. However, the patient died that day anyway. But it was not because of anything Laurens had done."

Dr. Boekman shook his head sadly. "Laurens must have thought he killed the man. When I reached home that night, my boy was already gone. Poor Laurens!" sobbed the doctor, brokenhearted. "Too afraid to contact me for all these years! How he must have suffered!"

Hans sought to lighten the doctor's burden. "Don't worry, we'll find him. I'm sure Father will soon remember the boy's name and where he can be reached."

The doctor brightened. "You'll send word the minute you have the faintest idea of where he said he would be?" the doctor asked. The Brinkers nodded yes. Dr. Boekman then said good-bye and went home a happier man than he had been for years.

At last, the day of the grand skating race arrived. The weather couldn't have been better—clear and bright. Already a huge crowd had gathered along the canal to watch. They had come from cities near and far. It seemed no one wanted to miss the excitement.

Down on the ice, forty boys and girls darted swiftly about on their skates. They were getting warmed up for their race across the ice. High spirits rang through the crisp, winter air as everyone waited for the race to begin.

Finally, the rules were read aloud: The girls would race first, then the boys. They would race a half-mile up to a marker, turn around, and come back to the starting point. There would be at least two races for each group, and the winners would be the boy and girl who had each won twice.

Many of the girls thought Hilda van Gleck would win, or perhaps a pretty girl named Katrinka, or the proud but popular Rychie Korbes. No one paid much mind to Gretel, who was wearing her red jacket and a new petticoat.

Carl Schummel was sure that he would win among the boys. Ben Dobbs had been practicing ever since he lost the practice race to Peter. Lambert van Mounen knew it would be tough beating Peter today, especially with so many people rooting for him.

Soon a bugle sounded and the girls lined up. The referee stood poised, then shouted, "Ready, set, go!" The racers were off in a blur of color and the crowd burst into cheers. It was hard to tell who was ahead immediately. At first, it seemed Katrinka was leading. But then Hilda shot past her, with two others close behind. Suddenly, a flash of red took the lead. It was Gretel! "Go, Gretel, go!" Mr. Brinker called out, spurring Gretel onward. In what seemed only seconds, the first race was over and Gretel Brinker was declared the winner.

While the girls rested, the boys lined up. The referee stood to the side once again and shouted, "Ready, set, go!" And the boys were off like a shot! The cheers of the crowd rang in their ears. Though there were only twenty racers, it seemed like three hundred legs were flashing by in an instant. It wasn't long before different boys took the lead. First, Ben had it. Then Peter overtook him. And then, Hans passed them both to forge ahead. His lead didn't last long, however, as Peter quickly caught up with him. Soon Hans and Peter were racing side by side, ahead of the others.

For a while, it looked as though the race might end in a tie. But in a sudden burst of speed, Carl drew aside and then bolted past Hans and Peter to win the race.

In the second girls' race, Gretel took an early lead. But midway through the course, she started to tire. Hilda soon overtook her and edged her out to win the race. The second boys' race saw Carl Schummel trip and fall halfway through the course. The other boys whisked around him, with Peter and Hans taking the lead. A few yards from the finish line, Peter lunged ahead of Hans to win the race.

The girls lined up for the third time, the referee gave the signal, and they were off once more. The crowd was cheering and shouting louder than ever. Calls such as "Faster, Rychie, faster!" and "Go, Hilda, go!" and "You can do it, Katrinka!" rang through the air. Through the noise, though, Gretel could hear her family's cheers for her. She was determined to win for them. Her quick, slender form soon sped past Rychie, Katrinka, Hilda, and the other girls. Gretel barely remembered turning around at the marker. All she knew was that she could not stop until she had passed the goal.

"Hurry, Gretel!" shouted Hans. Then Gretel dashed across the finish line. She had won the silver skates!

Hans looked to see if Peter had seen his sister's triumph, but Peter was working hastily at his skate. "The race is over for me now," said Peter, greatly disappointed. "I just tried to tighten my skate, and my lace broke." Without hesitating, Hans took the lace off one of his own skates and gave it to Peter. "I can't take that, Hans," said Peter, "though thank you for offering!"

Hans insisted. "Please, Peter. We're friends, and I'm badly out of practice. You must take it!"

"Come on, Peter!" called Lambert from the line. "We're waiting for you." Peter graciously accepted the lace from Hans.

Once again, the boys lined up and waited for the referee's signal. The split second they got it, the skaters were off, streaking across the ice. Hans watched, wishing all his speed and strength into Peter's feet. "Fly, Peter, fly!" he cheered. Hans's shouts mingled with the crowd's.

This third race among the boys was the most intense of all. Carl took the early lead. But then Peter skated past him. With the others in hot pursuit, Peter held his lead and crossed the finish line first. He had won the race— and the silver skates!

That evening, the Brinker cottage was in a festive mood. A fire blazed in the chimney. Warming themselves in front of it, the Brinker family chatted happily about the day's events. Suddenly, Mr. Brinker stood up and danced, snapping his fingers and kicking up his heels. "Hurray!" he shouted. "I've got it! The name is 'Thomas Higgs'! That's the name the boy wanted his father to write to!"

There was a knock at the door. "Maybe it's Dr. Boekman," Mrs. Brinker said, clapping joyfully.

It was not the doctor at all, but Peter, Lambert, and Ben. The three were on their way to a lecture, but had stopped so Peter could return the borrowed skate lace to Hans. "You did me a big favor," Peter told Hans. "I could never have won without your lace."

Hans blushed a little. He was relieved when Ben changed the subject by putting something on the table.

"This is the case for Gretel's silver skates," Peter said. "She ran off before the judge could give it to her."

The skate case was made of soft, red leather elegantly trimmed with silver. Daintily inscribed on the cover were these words: FOR THE FLEETEST. Inside, the case was lined with velvet, and in one corner were stamped the name and address of the maker.

Gretel thanked Peter and admired the beautiful case. "It's made by a Mr. Birmingham," she said.

"Birmingham?" said Lambert. "That's a place in England. Let me see." He examined the case and said, "Hmmm! Yes, you see, the case was made in Birmingham. The maker's name is in these small initials."

Peter squinted and read, "T. H." Turning around, he was surprised to see Mr. Brinker and Hans talking excitedly. Gretel was looking wild and Mrs. Brinker was rushing around, urging Hans to leave for Dr. Boekman's at once.

"That's it!" Mr. Brinker was shouting. "Thomas Higgs, in Birmingham! That's where the lad said to write!"

Then Ben spoke up, with Lambert translating for him. "Thomas Higgs, you say? Why, I know the man. His factory is not four miles from my home in England. He's a strange fellow, very quiet, and not much like an Englishman. But he makes beautiful things."

Hans rushed to tell Dr. Boekman the news of where his son was living. The doctor set off for Birmingham, England, at once. There he found his son, Laurens, who had changed his name to Thomas Higgs. Their long-awaited, father-son reunion was one of pure joy. And together, they returned to Holland.

Some time later, on a snowy day in January, Laurens Boekman went with his father to visit the Brinker family. In the short time since his son's return, Dr. Boekman's face had changed. He looked so much younger and brighter than before. The hard lines actually seemed to be melting away.

"I'm a happy man, Mr. Brinker!" said the doctor, laughing. "At last, I have my son home again. Laurens is going to open a warehouse in Amsterdam!"

Hans was surprised. "A warehouse? Won't Laurens be your assistant?"

"No," replied the doctor a little sadly. "He has no interest in medicine anymore. He wants to be a merchant."

Hans was truly amazed. "But the other calling is so much nobler! To be a surgeon, to cure the sick and crippled, to save human life and do what you did for my father—that's the grandest thing on earth!"

The doctor looked at Hans warmly. "Medicine is a difficult business, my boy. It requires great patience and hard work."

"And wisdom too!" said Hans enthusiastically. "And a deep respect for life. I'm sure it has its problems, but— " Hans stopped, for Dr. Boekman had suddenly turned to his son. Hans felt ashamed, fearing he had spoken too boldly.

Dr. Boekman then turned back to Hans and asked, "Would *you* like to become a physician, Hans Brinker?"

"Oh, yes, sir!"

"You would not grow restless and change your mind, just when I had counted on making you my successor?"

"No, sir. I would not change my mind," said Hans. Mrs. Brinker nodded her consent.

The doctor smiled and said, "If your father also agrees, then I would like to begin your training. Of course, I will gladly pay the cost of it. It will be like having two sons!"

Mr. Brinker smiled and said, "I prefer an outdoors life myself and look forward to working on the dikes again. But if Hans wants to be a doctor and has the chance to work for you, Doctor Boekman, it's all right by me."

Hans was so happy that he did not know what to say. Gretel looked up at her brother, sad that she would hardly see him once he went off to school. But, oh, was she proud of him!

Doctor Boekman and Laurens soon said goodnight and headed back to the city. The Brinker family stood waving from the doorway. Mr. Brinker looked proudly at his wife and two children. And as snow started to fall gently over the countryside, each of them knew they had much to be thankful for.